Angus Management

And the Missing Squirrels

1

Angus Management is an Animal Detective extraordinaire. He is the finder of lost socks, the guardian of lost people and the go to guy for any mystery or puzzle in Hellenge Hill.

4

Jimmy Bob – the Peacock has a problem, he is looking after the squirrel children today as the mummy and daddy squirrels have the winter larder to stock with nuts. The children have all gone missing.

Foxy the Fox has just moved in to Hellenge Hill. The quiet and peaceful animals have never had a predator on the hill. Jimmy is frightened that Foxy may have eaten the squirrel children.

Jimmy cries, "Angus if I have lost the squirrel children and they have been eaten by the fox then the mummy and daddy squirrels will be really sad. They will throw nuts at me and ruffle up my beautiful feathers!"

Angus comforts Jimmy, "Don't worry Jimmy, I will find this Foxy and if she has hurt a hair on any squirrel child's tail I will chase her away." Angus gets out his note pad, "now Jimmy, tell me the facts." He licks his pencil and looks at Jimmy.

Jimmy tells the story, "Well, the squirrel children arrived at 4am," all the animals on Hellenge Hill get up very early, that is how they stay fit and healthy. "They had brushed their teeth and combed their tails and they all had their books with them for school."

13

"I made blueberry porridge and some toast and the children ate quickly, they wanted to get out and play before Mrs Willow started the classes."

Mrs Willow was the school teacher. She was a very strict Badger, with a wonky nose.

"20 minutes later I could hear no noises, so I went to look for them. I met Tom the Sheep first – he was busy counting clouds trying to take a morning nap."

"I haven't seen anything but clouds," Tom answered, "750,000 of them."

"So, I went to see May the Heifer." Said Jimmy.

"I have been in the parlour delivering the milk and am far too busy to notice baby squirrels."

"She had always been a bit important for a cow," thought Jimmy.

Caroline the Chicken clucked by, "morning you two – Mrs Willow is looking for the squirrel babies, Jimmy, will they be in class soon?"

Jimmy began to cry, lovely Angus smiled. "Now then Jimmy, chin up, all things are safe and happy on Hellenge Hill. I think I already know where the squirrel babies are."

24

Jimmy looked at Angus with big eyes and through his tears he said, "but how, Angus, there isn't a clue anywhere in my story."

"No Jimmy there isn't, but there is a trail of blueberries right behind you and they lead to the new den of Foxy the Fox."

Jimmy screamed a loud and piecing scream and the blueberries, Caroline and Angus shook in their boots. "Calm down Jimmy," warned Angus.

At that point out of the hole popped a beautiful fox face with long eyelashes "good morning new neighbours, how kind of you to send the children to welcome me. How did you know that my favourite breakfast was ….."

Everyone stopped in their tracks – they thought that the fox had eaten the squirrel babies for breakfast.

"Blueberry porridge and toast!" Laughed Angus and out from the hole popped all the squirrel babies smiling and laughing and telling jokes to their new friend.

"Come on now" grinned Foxy. And all the animals saw that she didn't have a tooth in her head. "Time for school – but before you go make sure you brush your teeth again otherwise you will have to have false ones like me."

Angus smiled a special smile at Foxy and the world around them, faded away....

Angus Management

And the Rescue at the Sluice Gate

Angus Management is an Animal Detective extraordinaire. He is the finder of lost socks, the guardian of lost people and the go to guy for any mystery or puzzle in Hellenge Hill.

Angus was on the turn for home after a night on patrol around Hellenge Hill. He sped silently along the man-made river towards the sluice Gate. The sluice Gate allows water to travel from one end of the river to the other. They are large, metal gates that loom high out of the water and clunk noisily as they open and close. When they are open a torrent of water travels through them like water falling out of the biggest tap in the world. It is a frightening and dangerous place.

In the water below him he sees the fastest flash of silver as a giant pike swims with everything he has got towards the gate. The pike is moving super-fast and every muscle in his silver body is visible as he flexes his way through the water. Angus knows this Pike, his name is Grimacy Sideface and he is the most feared animal in the river at Hellenge Hill. He is also the kindest and Angus owes him his life.

Angus thinks back to a day when he was trapped in the reeds at the side of the river. He had been trying to rescue a duckling that had paddled too far away from his mother. Water is not a natural place for an owl to be and he was sinking, being dragged down by the sticky mess of plants that provide home to the animals who live half way in and half way out of the water.

Out of the corner of his eye he saw an otter who thought that Angus would make a tasty dinner. The otter was heading towards Angus with a hungry look in his eye when out of the water jumped the biggest fish Angus had ever seen. He knocked the otter back on the bank and it ran away under a low hanging tree; screaming it's head off.

48

The fish the lifted Angus with his tail and flipped him to the side of the river – like an owl shaped pancake. Angus gathered his breathe and thanked the fish. "I am Grimacy Sideface," said the fish, Angus noted that part of the fish's face was scarred and this meant he talked out of only one side of his big fishy mouth. "I am a Pike, and I look after the river and all who live here". Angus had introduced himself and the two had become friends. Grimacy Sideface was the wisest person that Angus had ever met. Angus gave him a nick name – Professor!

As these thoughts rushed through his mind he could see the drama unfolding beneath him. Grimacy was racing to the closing sluice gate and trapped between the gates, by a discarded plastic bag, was a little fish. "Hang on Sophie," called Grimacy.

The little fish cried and thrashed about, "help, I can't get free and the gates will close on me."

"Calm down," yelled Grimacy, "breathe deeply and swim in to the bag, I will make it Sophie – you will be fine, just stay calm."

The little fish took a breath and swam in to the bag. Grimacy Sideface redoubled his efforts and flicked his huge tail to get more speed, but the gate was closing and he was running out of time.

Angus saw a strong piece of wood sticking up from some old fencing. He puffed up his body and spread his wings. He grabbed the strong stick from the fence at the side of the river bank and just managed to get it into the closing gates before poor Sophie was squashed. The gates stopped.

At the same time Grimacy took a huge leap. Angus watched in awe as the fish flew through the air and grabbed the plastic bag containing the little fish and gently landed back in the water.

Just then there was a loud crack as the stick broke and the Sluice Gates finally closed.

Angus watched as Grimacy Sideface gently opened the bag and out swam little Sophie in to the river. "Thank you," she hugged Grimacy, "I could have died, you are the bravest, fastest and strongest fish in the river." Sophie swam back to her family. Her mother hugged Grimacy, and gave him a large bag of his favourite cakes.

Angus landed gently on a tree branch that over hung the river. Grimacy swam over "Thank you, Angus, that was really quick thinking, I would not have made the swim if you hadn't stopped the gates."
Angus was full of the type of pride you get when someone important gives you a compliment. "That's ok, Professor, I owe you about 50 times that."

Grimacy and Angus stayed together sharing the cakes talking about their adventures since they had last met and the world around them, faded away....

Angus Management

And the Chief of Police

Angus Management is an Animal Detective extraordinaire. He is the finder of lost socks, the guardian of lost people and the go-to guy for any mystery or puzzle in Hellenge Hill.

Today Angus was in a hurry, he was flying home to see Foxy. Angus had been to see his family on the other side of the trees, as a new baby had been born. He loved to visit his family, but he loved to get home.

Angus spun round the corner, flying low to catch Foxy and he bumped straight in to a pile of feathers. A gruff low voice came out of the mess of feathers and leaves, "Angus, why are you speeding around like a hog in a termite hill."

Angus had bumped straight in to the Chief of Police... Weg Liggling. Weg was a huge turkey from the Deep South of North America.

70

"Oh my goodness," flustered Angus, "I am so sorry Weg, I wasn't looking and, and..." "Angus, its ok what's got you all stirred up?"

Angus looked down at his feet, Weg was an imposing turkey and one of the most important people in Hellenge Hill, Angus was a bit embarrassed at being caught flying too fast.

"I was just on my way home to see Foxy.."
"Darn it Angus!" Weg interrupted, "I knew there was a woman involved. Always is when a guy is speeding, it's like night following day. Well I should rope you to a tree and feed you to the hornets but on this occasion, I am busier than a chook in a corn field and I need to get me and the boys busy locating a real bad guy."

At that point Angus looked around and 30 curious turkeys trotted out of the woodland. Angus smiled "morning all." There was an up roar of Turkey style "good mornings" back at Angus.

"Well Angus, I am all done here if you are; we will get on our way," drawled Weg.
Angus said, "Hey Weg, thank you for the caution, sorry I knocked you over. To make it up to you, maybe I can help."

"Now Angus, I know you are craftier than a whole cart load of cayotes, but you were already in a hurry."

"No that's fine, let me help. It's the least I can do."

Weg scratched his head and looked at Angus. "Well you are a hard man to refuse Angus. May the Heifer has had her bell stolen, well she thinks it was stolen, but that cow is dizzier than a bumble bee in a jam jar. We are checking the stoat's and weasel's hideouts, and then we are working our way around to the other side of the woods."

Angus grinned a huge grin "Well Weg, this is one I have solved before – follow me." "Wagons Ho troops," called Weg and 30 turkeys followed him out the woods.

The funniest sight greeted Foxy as she looked out of her front door; Angus, Weg and 30 police turkeys came walking across the field.

"Hey Foxy," shouted Angus, "are you free to give the boys in blue a hand with a mystery?"

Foxy laughed, "always a pleasure, Angus, what seems to be the trouble?"
"May and her lost Bell," winked Angus.

Foxy grabbed her coat and followed the rest of them off on to the Hill.

Angus led everyone to the water trough in the corner of May's paddock.

Foxy reached in to the trough, everyone thought she would pull the bell out from cold water but it wasn't there! Foxy looked at Angus, Angus grimaced, "but it's always there."

Weg laughed, "well Angus sometimes it's hard being a detective, let's go and do some real police work." Angus scratched his head. "Time to go and speak to that dizzy May again" drawled Weg.

Angus, hunch shouldered, followed Weg across the field. Foxy put her arm around him, but hid a smile behind her hand. Angus was never usually wrong!

"Aw my lady May," charmed Weg, "I have asked the great detective Angus Management to help me with the quest to find your bell."

Angus looked up, "hi May."
"Oh, I am so pleased you are home Angus you usually find my bell straight away."

"Dear Lady, your bell usually drops in to the water trough but it's not there, is there anyone who objects to your bell, or anyone who would really love one?"

May Shrugged her shoulders, "everyone loves my bell they miss the clanking sound it makes."

"Shusssssh" said Angus "listen." Everyone cupped a hand to their ear and listened clank, clank, clank.

"Oh," said Foxy "I can hear May's bell coming around the corner." Into view came Jimmy Bob the Peacock proudly wearing May's bell.

"Young Man!" Shouted Weg Liggling, "is that the bell that belongs to my friend May?"

"Oh!" said Jimmy Bob. "I just found it and I didn't know it belonged to anyone."

"Did you find it in the water trough," asked Angus. "Yeah, I like to look in it at my reflection in the water and there it was."

Angus laughed "She gets it caught on the side, but it's always there in the trough, normally she just comes over to my tree and lets me know but with me being away an all!"

Weg looked sideways at Angus conscious of the cheeky "an all" in a southern drawl. "Hoots mon" he exclaimed, and 30 turkeys and Foxy fell about laughing.

"Come on then troops, let's get this bell back on that cow," barked Weg Leggling. And 30 police turkeys lined up in pairs. "Angus, it's been great to bump in to you again – next time can you be a bit more gentle?"

This time Foxy looked confused and now Angus laughed and the world around them, faded away...

Angus Management

And the Gooseburry Thief

Angus Management is an Animal Detective extraordinaire. He is the finder of lost socks, the guardian of lost people and the go to guy for any mystery or puzzle on Hellenge Hill.

It was the middle of September on Hellenge Hill and the animals were getting ready for the Harvest Home celebration. Angus was tired, the summer had been busy for the detective as many people had been visiting the forest and eating picnics. The animals had been excited to see them but it meant that there were a lot of mysteries to be solved and questions to be answered.

Heather the Hedgehog was tending her garden; she was a keen gardener and always took prizes in the 'best in show' categories for strawberries and raspberries. This year she was excited about a new addition to her garden, gooseberries!

The gooseberries had appeared almost overnight on an old green bush in the corner by a large tree. Heather had been really surprised and delighted. She made a special mixture of sugar and water and sprayed the green shiny berries every day. As the sun had warmed them they had grown bigger and stronger.

Zak the Dormouse popped his head over the fence, "Hi Heather, are they gooseberries? My they look nearly ripe and good enough to eat".

Heather spun round and glared at Zak, "you keep your beady eyes of my gooseberries," she growled.

Zak's whiskers drooped and he pouted, "I was only trying to be nice and make conversation." He slunk off for a sleep in his favourite place to recover from the harsh remark.

Mrs Willow the local school teacher, came in through the back gate and startled Heather. "Oh my goodness, Mrs Willow, you gave me quite a start!"

"So sorry," said Mrs Willow, "I just wanted to get a sneaky peek at your entries for the Harvest Home."

Heather spread her arms out behind her and covered the gooseberry bush. "Oh no you don't, you be off and see them tomorrow." Mrs Willow thought Heather a little rude but smiled and left the way she came in.

Heather spent the whole day in the garden – talking to the plants and singing them songs while she sprayed them with the sugary mixture. "Sneaky Zak, bothersome Mrs Willow," she muttered to herself, "I don't need a friend in the world just the sunshine and my garden."

In the morning she woke up bright and early to go and collect her best berries for the show. "Morning strawberries, morning raspberries, morning goose……" oh no, all the gooseberries had gone. With her pinny still on and her hat ribbons flying around her head she ran to see Angus to ask him to begin an investigation.

Angus was trying to have a lie in; he got out of bed and put his dressing gown on then made his way wearily to the front door. Heather had run around his house three times by the time he opened the door and was jumping up and down frantically shouting, "someone has stolen my gooseberries."

Angus invited her in and put the kettle on - "strawberry tea should calm her down," he thought.

Heather sipped her strawberry tea and began to breathe normally again. She told the story of her visits from Zak the Dormouse and Mrs Willow.

She was so sad that the needles that normally stood up straight and prickly on her little body hung down in a dejected, sad, sorry for herself way.

Angus dressed quickly and went to Heather's garden, sure enough there was not a gooseberry on the bush. "Well Heather what do you think has happened?"

"It's clear to me that either Zak or Mrs Willow has been in and stolen them. I did speak to them harshly. I wish I hadn't!" sighed Heather

Angus summoned Zak and Mrs Willow; he also asked Ben the Beaver to join them. Ben was an expert on all types of trees and bushes and perhaps he could shed some light on the mystery.

"Zak and Mrs Willow," interrogated Angus sternly, "where were you between the hours of 8pm yesterday evening and 6am this morning." Zak explained that he had spent the evening with his best friend Tom the Field Mouse and Mrs Willow was at home because she had been looking after Luca the baby Penguin. "Both alibis are verifiable," Angus snorted, "I think you have some apologising to do Heather."

Ben and Angus went in to a huddle at the side of the garden. Heather apologised to Zak and Mrs Willow who forgave her straight away and comforted her by the carrots.

"I have solved the mystery," declared Angus, "Heather – this is not a gooseberry bush." Everyone gasped and looked at Ben and Angus, "this, my friends is an old Elderberry Bush, the perfect place for caterpillars to turn in to butterflies. Your gooseberries were cocoons. Look up in to the big tree Heather, what do you see?"

"Oh my, look at those, the most beautiful gooseberry butterflies in the world ever!"

Everyone was mesmerised by the butterflies, and the world around them, faded away....

Angus Management

And the Battle with Bleadon Hill

Angus Management and the Battle with Bleadon Hill

Angus Management is an Animal Detective extraordinaire. He is the finder of lost socks, the guardian of lost people and the go to guy for any mystery or puzzle in Hellenge Hill.

Simon the sneaky Stoat crept slowly through the night. He was in Heather the Hedgehog's garden and was picking away at the berries and putting them in a sack around his back. He counted as he went. Simon went next to the vegetable patch and began to slip some carrots and tomatoes in to his bag.

Behind Simon lingered Jerry the Rabbit. He also had a sack, and was in Mrs Willow, the school teaching Badger with the wonky nose's, garden, taking apples and pears from the fruit trees.

Hot on their trail was Angus, he flew gently on silent wings and landed in a tree above the heads of the two thieves.

Angus saw his friend Foxy the Fox and flew down to see her on the ground. "Are you watching that pair too," whispered Foxy, "lets jump them and make an arrest."

Angus looked sideways at Foxy and said, "shall we wait and see what they do with the loot first Foxy."

"But they are stealing, Angus, from our friends and neighbours. We should stop them right now!"

She tried to walk towards the naughty pair but Angus grabbed her by the tail. "No Foxy! Wait!"

Angus and Foxy followed Simon and Jerry back across the dark road that separated Hellenge Hill from Bleadon Hill.

There were excited noises as they came to a clearing on Bleadon Hill. All of the animal residents were waiting, with young and old animals at the front of the queue.

Simon and Jerry handed out the food and everyone ate. One tiny little mouse began to cry, "I wish we could grow our own food, but the rocky ground won't let us."

Foxy looked humbly at Angus and they headed back to Hellenge Hill. When they got back they called all the animals to a meeting. As they spoke about their discovery the faces of the animals went from angry to sorry.

Jimmie Bob the Peacock looked up and said, "we cannot just give away food, I know if I was them I would be too proud to accept it! We must find a way to help these animals help themselves."

Angus looked around at the worried faces in front of him, he smiled as a new idea came to him. "Let's have a market!"

"You want us to what!!" Mooed May the Heifer, "what is a market?"

Foxy looked up, "we all make things or bring food that we have grown and we swap it with the Bleadon Hill animals, for things that they have made or grown."

"But the Bleadon Hill Animals don't have any food," said Tom the Sheep, "what do they have that they can swap?"

"Rocks," said Angus, "well for starters, then I am sure they will begin to think of other interesting things that they have on Bleadon Hill that we don't have on Hellenge Hill."

The next day as Angus flew round Hellenge Hill he could see all of the animals making preparations for the market.

He stopped by to see Tom. Tom was excited; normally he counted clouds and aimed to get some sleep but not today. Today Tom was very busy; he was a great artist and was painting beautiful pictures to swap at the market. On each picture was a piece of his fleece. "These pictures are wonderful," smiled Angus. "Do you think you could make some posters for the market so that we can advertise it to everyone around?"

Tom puffed up his chest with pride, "wow Angus, I would love to." Nick the Magpie flew down, "I will put them up for you – all around the village." "Thanks Nick," said Angus, "that would be very kind."

Angus flew past the garden of Heather the Hedgehog, "Hi Heather," he shouted. Heather looked up "Hey Angus, look at this lovely rhubarb, I am so excited about the market." "See you there," called Angus and he headed home for a nap.

Ben the Beaver made his way across to talk to the beavers that lived on Bleadon Hill. He asked them if they were coming to the market. Sasha, the Bleadon Hill Beaver sighed, "what would we bring to a market." "Well," said Ben, "the animals on Hellenge Hill don't have any rocks to help build walls around burrows. We don't have any blackberries and I am sure there are other things you could trade too."

"Ooo," smiled Sasha, "all the pine is on our hill too and that makes a lovely tea and soft beds."

The day of the market arrived, the animals gathered in the clearing and began to lay out blankets for their stalls.

The animals with gardens had put together a fantastic spread of fruit and vegetables. Tom the Sheep had some beautiful paintings. Jimmie Bob the Peacock had made some very pretty pens from his feathers.

As they excitedly set up, they turned and noticed Simon the Stoat and Jerry followed by all the other animals from Bleadon Hill. Simon had rocks, Jerry had some beautiful cloth made from hemp, Sasha had baskets woven from the willow tree.

The animals excitedly traded with each other. "Three rocks for some rhubarb," bargained Heather the Hedgehog.

Angus and Foxy sat in the outdoor café with a glass of strawberry tea each, "well done clever Angus," smiled Foxy, and the world around them, faded away....

Angus Management

And the Tree Top Track

Angus Management was an Animal Detective extraordinaire. He was the finder of lost socks, the guardian of lost people and the go to guy for any mystery or puzzle in Hellenge Hill.

One Sunday afternoon Angus was just rising from sleep, he was looking forward to a blueberry porridge breakfast created by his best friend Foxy and a slow start to his evening routine when out of nowhere he heard a loud crash – followed by a long low scream.

He looked out of his doorway at the top of the tree and saw Brian the Badger hanging on a branch about six foot in the air.

Brian was an inventor and a bit of a thrill seeker – he was often coming up with new ways to throw himself about in the woods on Hellenge Hill.

Angus flew down to see if Brian needed any help, as he arrived Foxy was moving a broken branch closer to Brian so that he could climb down – or rather fall down a bit more safely.

"What are you up to now, Brian, why the Sunday afternoon din?" asked Angus, trying to sound as cross as he could and not laugh at Brian.

"Now Angus," Foxy interrupted "enough of the pointy talk, Brian is trying to make something for a very sick old squirrel."

"Interesting," mused Angus, "what are you aiming to do?"

"Ah now Angus my dear fellow," offered Brian as he landed softly on the ground, "Mrs McGonagall the Elder Squirrel has been bed ridden for three weeks with her sore hip.

On Wednesday, her grandson gets married in the wedding place by the old stones and she wanted to go.

I am working on an invention to get her across the trees – but struggling because it's a well-known fact that badgers are not great at climbing."

"Neither are Foxes," smiled Foxy, rubbing her rump.

"Come and look at the drawings, Angus," said Brian and he led him across to a makeshift table with papers spread on it. "The idea is sound but the execution is flawed."

Foxy smiled at Angus, "I wonder if you can find a way to help us build this contraption in to the trees."

178

Angus looked at the drawings, they resembled the old track of a tin mine he had seen in Cornwall once on his holidays only this time suspended in the air – and instead of carts on top of the track there were harnesses and seats dropping down underneath it.

"Mrs McGonagall can get into a seat in the harness and whizz down to the stones," explained Brian.

"What an amazing idea," said Angus, "but where are the materials?"

"Right here," Foxy smiled, "the beavers made everything – but they are not climbers either."

Angus looked at the materials and then up at the trees, he had a thought about how to make the idea even more exciting and he whispered something to Brian to ensure he had his approval, "of course, astounding!" Exclaimed Brian.

Angus put his wings in his mouth and whistled, a host of helpers flew from the trees including squirrels, birds and even some stoats. Angus gathered them together and explained what he wanted them to do.

Each animal had a part to play, some worked on the ground crew with Brian and Foxy, hammering parts together.

The birds flew up and down with the assembled pieces and the squirrels screwed them together in the air and prepared the branches.

The stoats worked hard with the beavers, making every piece just right and building a ramp at the edge of the wood that led high in to the first tree.

Ropes linked each tree together and there were several seats and harness combinations.

The track soared high and low and went round corners and loops to eventually end right by the wedding stone in the deepest part of the woods.

The animals worked happily together into the evening and the next morning when Angus was finishing his rounds, he saw the majestic site beginning to appear.

Banging and whistling carried on for two more days – Angus had to use his ear plugs to get to sleep during the day but he didn't mind – his excitement at the idea kept him in a good mood.

The evening before the wedding arrived and the animals waited eagerly to see if Mrs McGonagall could make the trip to the stones. She sat gently in to the harness on the seat and took her stick with her.

The harness whistled silently along the track, not stopping at all until the stones. At some parts it travelled quite quickly and Mrs McGonagall let out a little squeak. When she got off at the other end she smiled and hugged Brian.

"Brian, that was amazing, I will be able to see my grandson get married tomorrow and have a wonderful way of getting down while I am unwell."

"I am just glad it worked," said Brian, "and as Angus said, we can use it as a roller coaster when you don't need it!"

Angus blushed, "lots of animals in Hellenge Hill can't fly or climb, I just thought it would be great for them to have a way of feeling what that was like."

"You are so kind Angus," said Foxy looking slightly worried, "but maybe some of us just aren't meant to."

"Ooooooh Foxy," winked Angus, "not scared, are you?"

Foxy put her nose in the air, "of course not Angus."

"Well, let's go then" Mrs McGonagall got back in to the harness and Angus pulled her to the top of the tree to her home. Foxy and Brian walked up the ramp that the beavers and stoats had made and they arrived about the same time as Angus.

Foxy was unusually quiet as she slipped silently in to the seat, Angus sat next to her and put his arm around her "Don't worry Foxy, I have got you."

Foxy hid her head in Angus's chest and the squirrels released the break. Foxy and Angus screamed with joy as they began to hurtle through the woods. Just then it began to rain. "Rollercoasters in the rain," smiled Angus, "who ever said I wasn't romantic!" and the world around them, faded away....

Let's COLOUR!

Join Angus and his friends online:
www.angusmanagement.co.uk

Let's COLOUR!

Can you draw a proud peacock pattern
on Jimmy Bob's tail feathers?